The Wind in the Flute

Saal Baraan

ISBN: 978-1-7332708-8-5 (eBook)
ISBN: 978-1-7332708-9-2 (Print)

Book design by Luca Funari, *lucafunari@hotmail.com*

For all inquiries, please contact the author at:
XYZ Parenting LLC
2211 South Telegraph Road, #7346
Bloomfield Hills, MI 48302

Email: *saalbaraan@gmail.com*

www.authorsaal.com

Table of Contents

Foreword from the Author

Ultimately, readers decide what a book is about. For me, this book represents an abbreviated version of the many lessons I've learned through both positive and negative experiences in my adult life.

Here, you'll find wistful tales of wisdom and generosity that didn't cost much. Still, these instances generated precious moments of joy and of happiness for the people involved. Some events changed the course of otherwise hopeless circumstances.

Risks were taken that resulted in handsome rewards. Some decisions turned out to be foolhardy—a truism for all of humanity. Some of the outcomes and results remain unclear because we were not present to witness the way things turned out a few years down the road.

Within this book, you'll find stories in prose and prose poetry. Hopefully, you'll find my unique offerings entertaining.

Like my previous book, *Of Myriad Paths,* that conveyed the message of hope in hopelessness, *The Wind in the Flute* conveys an important message of learning through giving and by risk-taking. I am convinced that the book will inspire many of us to 'give' with fewer misgivings. The hardened human instinct often works toward self-preservation and communicates with logic, which often leans toward wealth accumulation and total self-protection. Yet, the best of life is saved for those who are magnanimous.

Giving means overcoming your fears of both scarcity and failure. By housing yourself in generosity, you will see lives changing—yours included. There is no better satisfaction than that feeling.

Hope you like the book,

Saal Baraan

Acknowledgements

I would first like to acknowledge Alina Tertychna for her superb skill in creating sketches for every story in this book. Her artistic talent and her understanding of the wisdom behind each story is something I sincerely appreciate.

I must thank and acknowledge Olivera Novitovic for designing the cover that attracts the eyes toward innocence and light spread with music in the air.

Thanks to Matthew Kirkpatrick for his significant contribution in editing and proofreading. Matthew was painstakingly thorough and diligent.

And to Lee Caleca for the final copy edit of this book.

Thanks to beta-reader Corinne Fox for her invaluable guidance and candid thought-provoking questioning. I very much appreciate it.

Last but certainly not least, I wish to thank my daughters, Zoha and Aleesa, for always encouraging me to write. They don't mind listening to me rattle on about my writing projects. They are the treasures of my heart.

Finally, my mother for being there for me through all my formative years.

This book is lovingly dedicated to my father and my wife.
Their generosity of spirit far exceeds my own.

The Wind in the Flute:
A Prayer

Let me be the wind that flows

Through the flute unabashed

To revive, to instill, to distill life.

Let me be the instrument of change

To empower, to brighten the downtrodden

To be an answer to their prayers

To be the hand that lifts the fallen.

Give me ears to truly listen, eyes to behold.

Give me courage to take a bet, a chance, a risk.

Let me be a windfall for the hopeless.

Let giving flow through me and me be,

A gift that that gives and keeps on giving.

Let me be more heart and less logic in giving.

Bring the selfless out of myself in being.

Let every chance encounter be a lesson.

Let courage guide my decisions.

Let generous be my spirit alone.

Let my judgement be suspended.

No shying away from the soul's wisdom.

Let me count once more

On the will of the beaten ones

To rise again with my gesture of hope.

Let me hear their flutes again.

Let me be the wind in them.

The Old Man and His Taxi

Dᴜʀɪɴɢ ʜɪꜱ ᴛɪᴍᴇ navigating the vibrant streets of Pakistan, Adil often journeyed by taxi. Rickshaws were cheaper, but he found them to be a pain in the back. Not just metaphorically speaking—but literally. He'd heard stories from other passengers claiming that when Rickshaws slammed into potholes at a certain angle, one's back pain could be cured. In his experience, however, the opposite was true—they caused more pain than they cured. A reverse miracle of sorts.

Aesthetically, most vehicles were painful to look at. No Cadillacs or luxury cars of any kind were available, that's for sure. Taxis often ambled through the pock-marked streets bereft of basic safety requirements like side-view mirrors, rearview mirrors, or windows altogether. Many of the things we take for granted here in the developed world were absent in Pakistan, a place of sound, sand, heat, and striving.

With that said, taxis took him from point A to point B and so met his basic transportation needs.

In his travels, he had encountered many unique drivers, each a solid caricature in their own right, with their own stories to tell. There were undoubtedly some interesting conversations that took place. This in part compensated for the lack of quality of their vehicles. Most drivers were from Northern Pakistan and held their presence with strong sentiments, full of convictions. They were short-tempered but good-natured, compassionate, and honest.

On one occasion, he hailed a taxi and, at first glance, was inclined to decline the car that stopped at his waving hand. Part of him wanted to say, "No, thank you, I don't want it," or even "Jao," which translates loosely to *just go*.

It wasn't any one specific thing. The taxi was cobbled together with found artifacts, missing bits and pieces everywhere as if it had once been devoured by a swarm of rabid moths.

Not just the fabric. This must have been a new species of moth that was hungry for the whole thing. He couldn't tell if the back door or trunk were functional. But then his eyes fell on the driver.

He looked to be in his 60s and had a genuine smile, someone who had been working honestly in this cab his entire life. Against his initial inclinations, he stepped into the cab and sat down.

Adil had a sinking feeling, literally; he was sinking in the seat, which almost bottomed out from under him. The cabbie started to drive. Adil felt that this was potentially the last ride this taxi might ever take: the death rattle of its final gasps.

His premonition was correct. Within a few miles, the taxi screeched to a halt. The driver reassured Adil that this often happened, so not to worry. He claimed he would make it run again and knew what to do.

He got out of the vehicle, popped open the hood, and got straight to business with his mechanical work. Adil didn't bother to move. He knew so little about how cars worked; he wasn't prepared to even try to pretend that he understood what he was supposed to be doing.

The car eventually choked to a start again, back to the land of the living, and with a happy face, the driver hopped back in and they continued toward Adil's destination.

A mile down the road, it stopped again. This time the driver looked concerned. Adil stepped out, having decided that he would pay the cabbie his fare, which was eighty rupees (about eighty cents), and then find another taxi.

He looked inside the car and saw the driver, red-faced and flustered fiddling with the ignition while kicking the clutch and brake and accelerator. He turned around to check his surroundings and saw that (by sheer luck) there was a car repair shop nearby. He pointed it out to the driver and told him that he should let the repair shop take a look at his car. The driver didn't answer; instead, he continued to fidget with different parts of the vehicle.

Adil had to tell him that he couldn't wait. He was itching to leave, to pay, and to get the transaction over with and find another cab. The driver, a man of strong principles, refused to accept any payment since he didn't manage to take Adil to his destination. This really touched Adil; he took out a bundle of cash—whatever he had at the time—and handed it over to the driver.

When he extended his hand to the driver, he looked at the hand, which held so much money, and he flashed with rage for a moment.

"Are you mocking me?" he asked.

"Absolutely not," Adil responded. "I want you to get your taxi checked out at the repair shop so you can get back on the road." Adil assured him that they needed to keep honest people like him on the road. He figured that if his taxi died permanently that day, the driver should be able to sustain his life, one way or another.

The driver was transfixed with the money in his hands. Adil heard the driver raise his voice, but he was long gone by then and didn't look back.

Twenty-Four Hours of Wait

She let her husband go
In wait of the pursuit,
The possibility of the news,
The news of the arrival.
The arrival of a baby, maybe
'The odds were against them,
But they had still parted,
Following false hopes.'
Mothers gave birth, failed to part.
Struggle indeed for bleeding hearts.
After giving birth, promises were lost.
Couples in waiting, stay disillusioned
Yet we've waited eagerly for so long.
Let's go back, I told my wife,
It's not our destiny, not in this life
Stop chasing a hopeless dream.
A path which was not our gift,
Turn back, return home.
She demurred, her gut feeling strong.
Leave the chance to adopt a baby? Not now.
We have come a long way to this land
Adoption, a grueling affair.
The odds are against us. You know?
I'll stay behind for a month here.

Call it a woman's intuition, she smiled.

Dejected, I left her to test her luck,

Crossed oceans alone in despair,

Present now in my place of bearing,

In my own home—buzz, buzz, buzz—

The phone ringing.

Hello! What? No, it's impossible.

Speechless and confused.

Twenty-four hours since I boarded that plane,

A baby softly cries beside her miles away

In the background; *no it can't be!*

Eyes moisten, my words inaudible.

Giggles from my wife on the other side,

My dear daughter, why did I leave?

This is not possible! Impossible!

How can it be?

That there lies this breathing beauty.

Alive, but not in my arms.

My hope diminished too soon.

One day too soon.

To miss my newborn by a day,

By twenty-four hours! For Goodness sake,

Months would pass before I would touch her,

Before we could meet in the physical realm

A split-second decision, to pay a price

That felt like a lifetime to me.

But I've won this lottery, so why whine

I accept the precious gift in absence.

The Disappearing Son

A week ago, I was watching an episode of *I Dream of Genie* with my daughter. It was the episode in which Genie tells her master that she is very upset. She explains that she does not remember her own birthday, which is no surprise since her birthday was somewhere around 2,000 B.C.

Every time Genie was sad, part of her physical body disappeared. Viewers first noticed the disconcerting sight of her feet and legs disappearing and then reappearing.

Last night, I felt my identity as a son undergoing a similar crisis when I took a visit to see my aging parents. My mother has dementia, but she did not have much trouble identifying me—that is, up until last night.

She has no recollection of my wife or my daughters. After six hours at my parents' place and having three meals with her, my mother asked me why I was still working with cars when I was so educated and not doing what I had studied to do.

I am a doctor by profession, and I do not deal with cars. I know nothing about cars. My father balked at this line of questioning as I slowly realized that my mother had mistaken me for somebody else. When we asked her who she thought I was, she stated I was her nephew.

My heart skipped a beat then and my stomach felt hollow as I realized that part of my identity as a son was disappearing. Whether we accept it consciously or not, external validations confirm various parts of our existence. My students make me a teacher; my children make me a father. You get the picture, right?

My father and I frantically tried to reignite those memories, which would bring my identity back. We reminded her that it was me, Sulaiman. Her son, a doctor. We reminded her of the role she played as the direct force and support behind me.

I reminded her of how I had honored her after my graduation, wrapping a white coat around her. A coat she still has saved in her closet. She recalled and recognized it, but I do not know how long it remained part of her memory. It came back for a fleeting moment. She suddenly remembered how mischievous I was as a child, telling stories about how I had climbed a tree once and fallen down.

I did not mind at all that I had been saved by my prior mischievous endeavors. Without those strong emotions to attach a memory to, half of my identity as a son was threatened with eradication. I was almost completely erased.

Later that night, teary-eyed, she told me, "When I look at you, I feel very happy inside that someone very close to me is here. It may be my brother, but how can it be?"

I remembered that my uncle had passed away many years ago. "It may be my sister's son, then."

I began to disappear again.

Month after month, with each of my visitations, my mother's memory and emotions fluctuated until one day she had a sharp and lucid recognition of me for which I wasn't prepared. She said suddenly, "You are my son! Oh my God, where were you for so many years?" The monologue went on. "How come no one told me you were my son?" I was speechless—happy that my mother recognized me, but also very sad that this was fleeting and would not last. "How come I have no memory of you? Did something bad happen to us?" I was deeply moved by her kindness, hugs, and kisses. Her love and prayers thereafter felt like a much-needed rain after a dry season. But I felt deep pity for her condition and anger at life's cruelty.

The tumultuous waves her mind is drowning in makes me a helpless spectator. It is particularly burdensome because I am supposed to be a healer and there is no treatment I can offer. I have a tapestry of conflicting emotions, but I am a mere brush and destiny the hand. "Why did you run away? Who took care of you for so many years? I am so sorry I wasn't there for you. Are you married?

Finally, I had a chance to answer, "You took care of me Momma. I never went anywhere; sometimes you become forgetful but now you remember. I know I should have told you (I do that every time but she doesn't register) that I was your son."

Then she cries and prays to God that all my worries and problems be taken away from me and given to her. She used to say that when we were young. And it felt that she really saw me this time—truly saw me—and I am so grateful for this lovely moment between a mother and son. We went over the old pictures in a family album and it was a joy.

Sometimes life is a sea of troubles with islands of joy. Look for an island.

Memory of My Hand

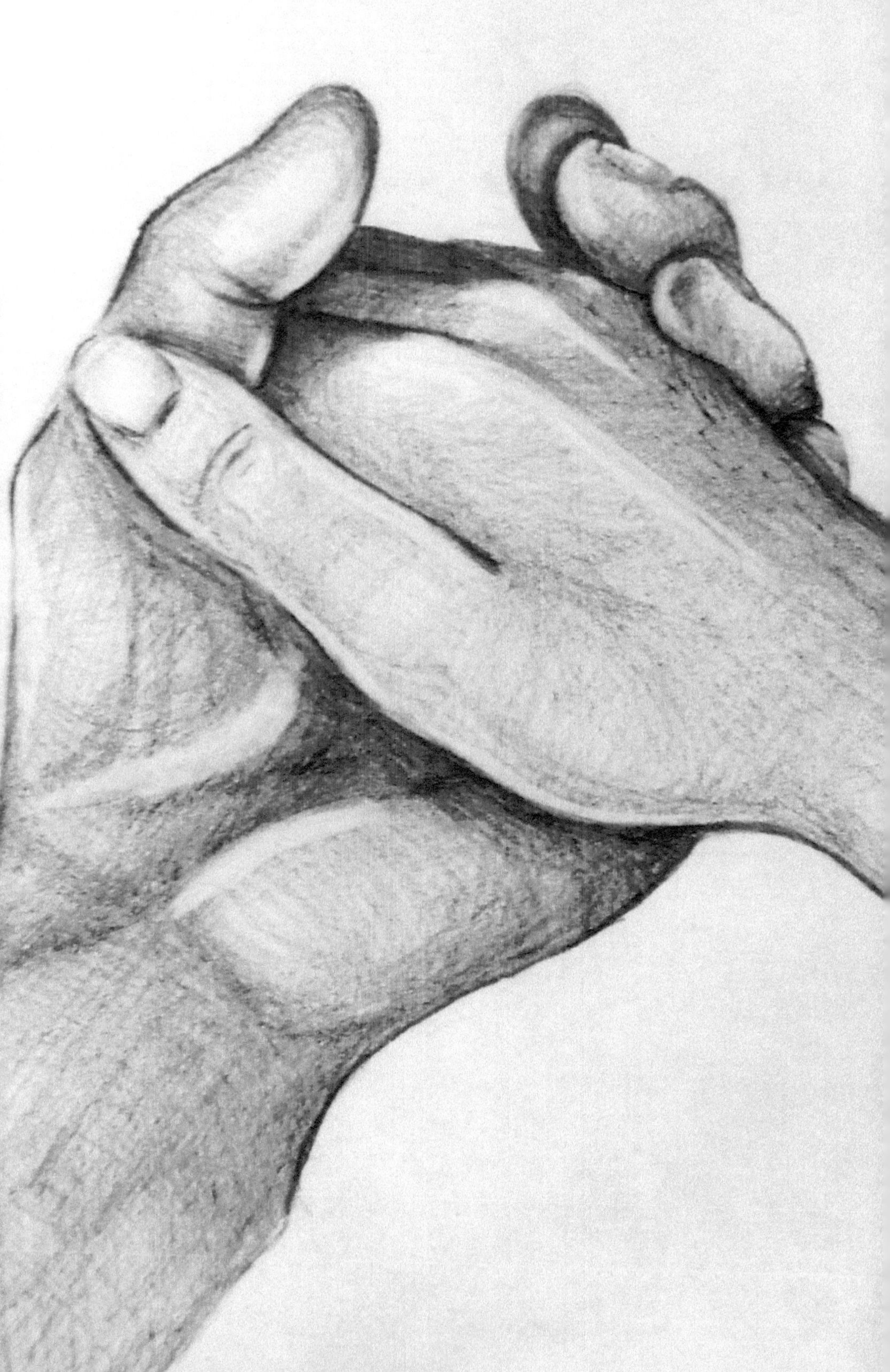

Soft tickle of butterfly dust
The silk of white linen petals.
Smooth caress of a woman's face,
Warmth of a hearth after a frost.
A velvet jacket hung in a closet
A grip of a bird's claws.
A wet nuzzle of a dog,
The fit of a fine pen within,
The sting of a fastball
Icy embrace of a cold glass
(After a hike in heat),
Clingy sand in a closed fist
A smooth oval rock.
Gestures for a hundred emotions,
The giver, the seeker
The helping, the feeding
The blessing and the rocking
And last, to share that all
A warm clasp of another.

In Praise of Crowdsourcing

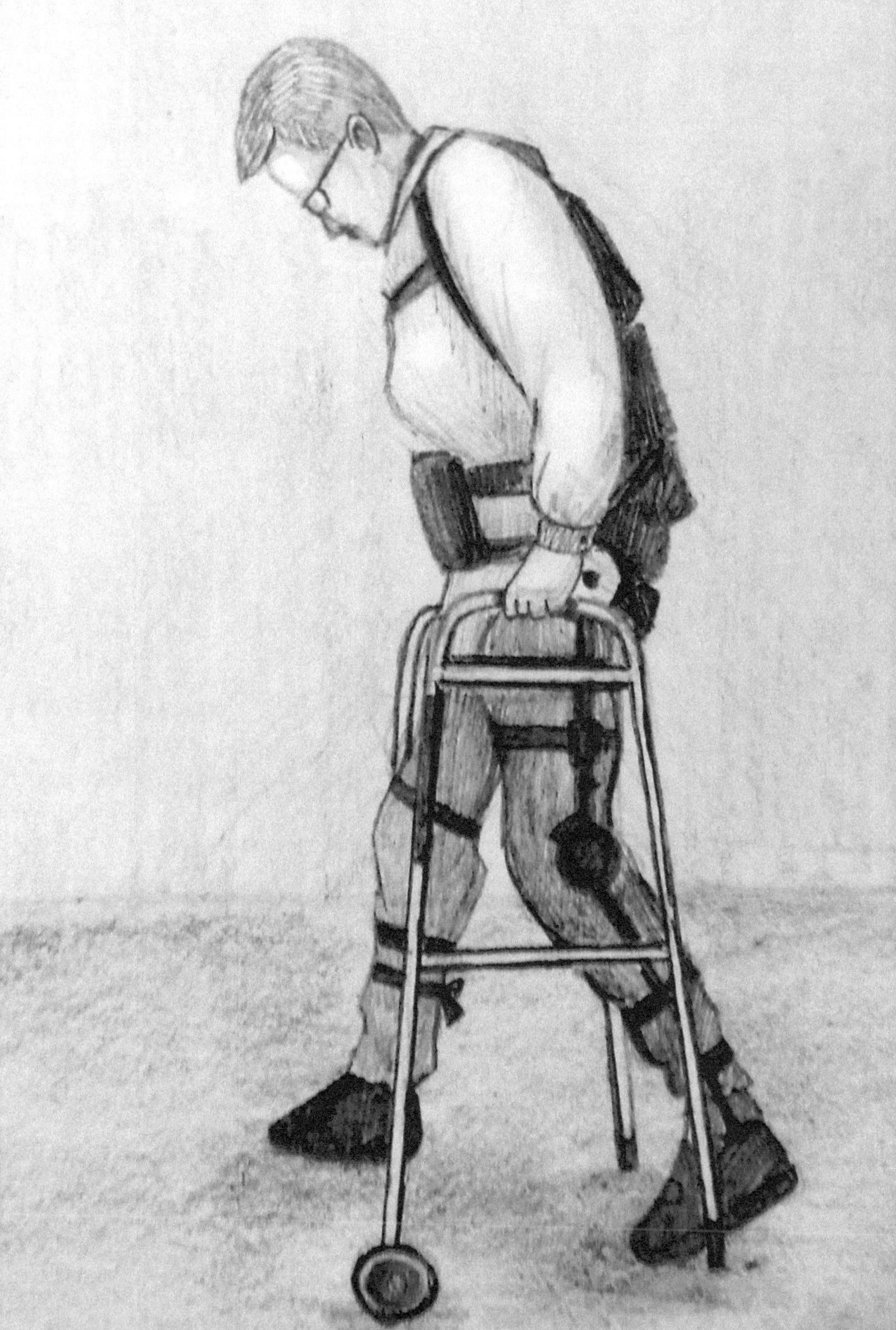

Call it a caregiver's wishful thinking,

The stroke that incapacitated him,

A clot that robbed us both of our beings.

His anger spared none, not me either.

An unexpected baby, born by me;

To his care went every step of mine,

My senses faded to rain, down from shine.

Then another unexpected happening,

A welcome gift by crowdsourcing.

Robot-assisted recovery plans,

Especially for him,

A maid for me, and nurses too.

Standing upright beside these machines

He could now look me in the eyes.

The robots move him by his commands,

Life's demands eased;

There is domesticity to our home once more

A vacation finally is in the works,

I cannot thank you enough, my folks,

The crowd, the fund, sourced a new life for us.

To Park a Trailer

Jerry helped Serena out with the yardwork in their Milwaukee home. Since she'd bought a foreclosed property, both the front and back yards were badly neglected. Serena was able to apply quite a few of her landscaping ideas with Jerry's dedicated hard work. Jerry was a daydreamer who would drift away into his thoughts while working. He planned on running a landscape business of his own one day.

He had dyslexia and borderline hearing loss. He lacked formal education, and he lacked the ability to plan. Plus, he didn't quite understand how to run a business. Still, that didn't stop him from purchasing two lawnmowers and a big bulky trailer to house them. The only problem was that he did not have a driver's license. Years ago, his license had been revoked under mysterious circumstances (Serena suspected DUI).

"Can I park my trailer in your driveway?" Jerry asked Serena one day.

"What's your plan, Jerry?"

"I'm gonna do the lawns in the neighborhood. I ain't got no place to put my trailer. The trailer park where my house is won't allow me to keep it." That was how it all started.

"So, why'd you buy it, Jerry?" Serena asked.

"I wanna store my lawn riders here."

"And why do you need two of them?" Serena was direct.

"I'm gonna have my business and I'm gonna need 'em both."

"Jerry, you have a cart before the horse situation here." Serena wondered if Jerry was following her. "You cannot drive and you don't have a truck or a truck driver to haul this trailer with two lawn mowers around."

"I have someone I'm talkin' with to be a partner in my business."

"Does he have a truck?"

"No, but he said he was gonna 'range for one."

"How long are you gonna park it here if I allow you to?"

"Maybe a month or so," Jerry answered.

"Okay, you can bring it here."

"How much are you gonna charge me, ma'am?"

"I don't need any money. Just figure out your life, Jerry".

Two years passed.

For two years that trailer remained in Serena's driveway as if she were the owner. Her husband Raj supported her decision, though not without a little resistance.

The workers renovating the home often complained that the trailer was in their way. Serena didn't pressure Jerry and instead asked the workers to work around it and move it a bit even if they had to hire an extra pair of hands.

Jerry showed up one day with someone. "This is Tom, my business partner."

"Hi Tom, how's life?" Serena sensed where this was going.

"Good, ma'am, thank you."

"My business cards—here ma'am, take a few. Please hand 'em out to people you know…"

"…and for Raj also," Jerry interjected.

So, Jerry had finally found a partner/driver and the truck to carry the trailer, and now they were ready to run a landscaping business. Serena was happy for Jerry and wished him all the success.

In the greater scheme of things, Jerry did not ask Serena a huge favor, and she hadn't done that much monetarily. But Serena often wondered where Jerry would have parked this trailer without paying a hefty fee. He was by all measures at or below the poverty level, and from what she knew he had maxed out his credit card on what he'd bought. It was a rash judgment on his part, and he literally had no cash to pay for the rent for storage of the trailer. It was an obstacle for Serena's family, but a breakthrough opportunity for Jerry. Serena was the proverbial wind in Jerry's flute, and he produced a few merry notes out of it, at least for the foreseeable future.

Seventy-Two Hours in London
Without a Visa

I wonder who let you board the plane, Sir?
Residents of your country require a stamp,
You arrived in London without one. Surprise!

I'd bought a ticket, showed my passport,
No such objections had been expressed,
By the ticketing agent.
Boarded the plane, I'd cleared security.

Now take the flight back to your country,
Without a visa you cannot be here;
It was an oversight, sir,
Not really your fault
Still, you'll be detained
Til the next flight out.
But, I have come for an invited talk!

Years of research packed within my case,
A discovery, ready to be shared,
I plead.
Please! Just let me share my work, my discovery
At this competition,
Which I am prepared to win.
The officer left with my papers

Time went by slowly, flights landed,
Flights departed.
My morning flight was ages ago.
Detention feels like this: time stops.
Limbo, purgatory, a decision pending
With consequences unknown,
The hidden fates
Left to the observer's imagination
Open to the judgement of passersby
What crime has he committed?
What has he been waiting for?
Or, *what lies in wait for him?*

Another officer returns to me
Face betraying neither hope, nor resignation
You have a talk tomorrow at noon?
Yes, I do sir, as per the agenda, true.
We will keep your passport.
You are free to go
Give your talk, you have 48 hours;
Return to the airport when done
Then pick up your passport from me.
You'll fly back to your country
The day after tomorrow's departure.
Kind nature, welcoming gesture,
Restored my chance to shine,
My focus shifted to my lecture.
Thank you, officer, you've made my day!
My talk received the first prize award.

Gentleman's word, I returned to the airport
Here's to you officer, my immense gratitude
Because of you I won a prestigious award.
Thanks for your precarious trust,
Taking a chance, thinking outside the box,
Beyond the rules, guided by just compassion.

Want to be a Nurse? Well, Maybe

MARY ANNE WORKED for the Lalanis as a nanny in Abu Dhabi. But the story is not really about her. It is about her seventeen-year-old daughter in the Philippines. Of course, Mary Anne missed her. Her daughter, Rayna, sounded like a sweet girl.

Mary Anne was liked by the Lalani family-Samir, Sara, and their children. Samir was a gentleman and a very compassionate person, and he took good care of Mary Anne. In return, Mary Anne took care of Samir's children like they were her own.

Samir saw that Rayna was brave and had grown up independently. She'd scored well in high school and wanted to be a nurse. Yet, sadly, that was out of the question since the tuition was unaffordable for their family. This is not an unusual story.

Samir and his wife Sara asked Rayna to find out about the tuition at the top ten universities in the Philippines for nursing. They encouraged her to apply to see if she at least could gain admission. To their pure excitement, she got into a very prestigious school. Samir and Sara became hopeful and showed high expectations once they made up their minds that they would provide tuition for Rayna.

The tuition was steep and equivalent to a university in a Western country. This process was also by no means easy. Samir was no fool. He first tried to arrange a direct deposit from his bank to the university registrar's office, but the university would not allow that. After much frustration, Samir finally sent a Western Union MoneyGram at the beginning of the school year every year.

Rayna would then pick up the money in cash and go straight to the school registrar to pay her enrollment fee. For obvious reasons, this arrangement was not to Samir's liking. He was concerned for her safety, walking through the streets of Manila with $7000 in cash.

There was no other option, though. Mary Anne did not trust her relatives back in Manila, so there was no adult in the equation.

Their fears subsided soon. After her first year, the principal's office reported her high scores and good grades.

Samir's initial arrangement with Rayna was that she would send him her grades every six months. The first report was very encouraging. Rayna's life would change, and she would be out of the clutches of poverty once she became a nurse.

Mary Anne showed her deep gratitude to the Lalani family. She doted on them and worked extra hard at pleasing them.

Samir and Sara felt generous and fulfilled that they could help where help might matter. A natural human feeling.

In the second year of Rayna's nursing school, Samir followed the usual protocol and sent the money. All was quiet after that. He did not get the mid-year mark sheet and asked Reyna to send her grades to make sure that she was still thriving and keeping up with the rigors and demands of her nursing school. To his surprise, he did not hear anything back. Mary Anne reported that Rayna was busy studying.

Time passed steadily, and still no word. Soon it was year three. Before sending the fees, Samir wanted to know about her grades. He was serious about the importance of good grades and education. Rayna was like his daughter now and he felt responsible for her future. He was disturbed, however, when he received (after so many requests), a fuzzy and unclear fax with some items scratched off. Naturally, this aroused his suspicion. Asking Mary Anne to check on Rayna was not helpful because Rayna sent a reassuring message that all was well.

Sara, however, took upon herself the task of locating Rayna on Facebook.

They were shocked to find Rayna's Facebook page full of posts of her and her friends dining at exquisite places, wearing fashionable clothes, and vacationing on the neighboring islands.

Now of course, there is no problem with a young girl taking a holiday with friends, but with no proof of Rayna's grades, Samir knew deep down that something wasn't right. He called the university financial services and they informed him, much to his horror, that Rayna was no longer enrolled at the university.

Sometime after her first year, she had dropped out. This is how it was revealed to the Lalanis that their effort to bring someone out of poverty through education had not materialized. Sadly, they weren't financing Rayna's education. They were financing her social life.

Needless to say, the next few weeks in the Lalani household were tense and upsetting. Mary Anne was in obvious grief and offered to reimburse the money from her salary. Samir, though hurt, wouldn't go this low. He finally reasoned himself out of this whole experience. Not without Sara's help, of course.

Some college experience is better than no college exposure. The intention may be clear, but the outcome may vary and may not be to his satisfaction. In the end, Samir tried to reach out to Rayna a couple of times to see if he could still get her back on track and in school. If that was what she really wanted, she deserved a second chance. She was very young still. However, Rayna refused to talk to him and blocked his phone number.

Samir later discovered that Rayna had followed a senior dropout from nursing school into the Call Center market. He sincerely hoped she would do well and find her own music.

Florida Blues

I sleep light, troubled by the sound and sight.

Total darkness and total quiet, are not an inalienable right.

Travel by the road makes decisions skewed.

With no advance booking you seldom choose.

Checked into a motel without reviews,

The music was loud, parties wild, we were ignored,

No class, no style; too tired to go search again,

The walls were porous, the security disrobed,

And the party got rowdier as

Midnight bowed its sleepy eyes;

Dreams were elusive, like the manager with flaws,

Too shy to intervene, to implement laws;

The youngsters, the hipsters, the bawdy, the brave,

Yelling across the halls somebody's name.

In jest and in total lack of shame

Stationed to chat outside our walls,

The frustration mounts within, anger rising.

We wait another hour for sleep, failing

To ignore the nasty inconsiderate lot, trying;

My kids woke up again, noise not diminishing.

A couple of rowdy girls—late teens, early twenties about,

Sitting on my window ledge, one tipsy, almost out,

Another stern, loud, hyper and quite cold;

I could see their silhouette through the blinds,

Saw them clear through the viewer peephole.

Two a.m., the thoughtless insensitive kind.

I took a step, replayed in my mind, a thousand times,

Opened the door to drive away the rowdy ones.

'We're trying to sleep here, go away, it's past bedtime'

What will u do? Call security, bitch? Go back inside.

Taken aback I responded in kind, a curse for a curse (mistake #2).

Before I blinked, the girls were on top of me, a riptide.

I haven't been in a fist fight since I was a little boy.

Angel dust, it must be their choice,

Their violence grew.

As I struggled to keep them away at arm's length

A hundred punches fell on my face and head.

The bloodied nose, the deafened ears, the broken tooth

The swollen head, drumming like rain

Dhup, dhup, dhup, dhup, dhup, dhup, dhup, dhup…

My loss of consciousness did not stop her zeal.

Sitting on my chest, her punches sculpted my face.

Peeled from my body by my spouse and her friends,

Shutting the door behind her was no relief for me.

In utter madness, she broke the grip of her friends,

Her mission to seek and destroy,

Like a heat-seeking missile, she returned

To knock down the windows, and my doors.

Driven by an unknown spirit, a lost warrior,

Her goal was to finish the job that night.

Her punches rolled on in the air when,

While lifted away for her own good,

For if caught tonight she is slated to spend

A part of life in prison, a mark forever,

Her imaginary punches were meant for me.

It took a crowd to carry her away.

Right before the policeman made his way,

I looked in the mirror, an unrecognizable face

Silence finally came, but with a price to pay;

Nine-one-one, gave explanation, the party at least stopped,

Assaulters visibly missing from the round-up,

Boys and girls all in a lineup, some wave hello.

I remember the face of my tormentor, cannot forget.

Innocence was lost by PCP and meth

I almost lost my life, worse is the psyche

My wife and kids were traumatized.

Wrong hotel, wrong move, wrong outcome.

Her frenzy could have ended me;

Am I to be blamed to ask for quiet?

Some peaceful place for sleep's sake?

Asking for peace put so much at stake

In Florida I should call 911 first I suppose.

Nine-one-one. What is your emergency?

People are having a party this late,

Loud noise is disrupting my sleep.

A couple of them are outside my room

Please use nine-one-one for real emergencies

Nine-one-one. What is your emergency, sir?

The couple outside have beaten me up.

They are breaking down my door.

Is it an emergency now?

One Donkey, Two Donkeys

CAB RIDES IN KARACHI allow for a closer glimpse of society both on and off the road. It is very common to come across donkey carts with either a single donkey or a pair cruising by, with enthusiastic riders who often transport both animate and inanimate products from one end of the city to another.

Javed had heard stories from his father about the donkey carts, but seeing them first hand was a fascinating experience. He'd grown up in the States and wanted to visit the land of his forefathers. But what he saw disturbed him.

The sad sight of the donkeys pulling enormous loads of cargo and hearing the animals cry in distress was not what he'd expected. That was not the part of the narrative he'd grown up with.

During one of his cab rides, he both saw and heard a donkey crying while carrying an enormous load uphill. Immediately, he asked his cab driver to pull over.

The rider got off his seat and hopped on the road next to the donkey to pull the cart and the donkey uphill. The cart wouldn't budge, but the rider didn't give up. The donkey brayed in distress. The locals have learned to tune out these sounds over the years from frequency of exposure.

Javed asked his cab driver if he would be willing to push the cart with his cab, and he asked the donkey rider to take some of that load off the poor donkey.

That was an awkward moment indeed, for both the taxi driver and the donkey rider looked at each other and then back towards Javed. The novelty of the request led to confusion and disbelief.

"Why don't you use two donkeys, to lighten the load?" Javed queried the rider. "At least then this poor donkey won't die from the toil and misery."

Unsurprisingly, the cart rider's response pertained primarily to the financial constraints. Fifty thousand rupees ($500 us) would be the cost of a new donkey.

"What if I were to buy you another donkey?" He asked the rider. With a big grin that was hard to suppress, the rider eagerly declared that it would be very generous of the gentleman.

"It's the least I could do for the poor creature," he thought to himself, feeling magnanimous. So at the spur of the moment, they set off to the Ghadda (donkey) Market near Bakra Piri. Apparently, the buying and selling of donkeys is a prosperous business, and it remains open until 10:00 PM.

By this time, Javed's taxi driver, who started off being amused, was now in total bewilderment. He was losing touch with reality. *His passenger wanted to go to the Ghadda Market to buy a donkey for a total stranger (who could be a crook) he spotted on the street. My passenger today is either stupid or insane. I hope he pays me the fare for driving him around.*

They all met at the market that evening. They found a healthy animal who would be a suitable companion for the cart rider's donkey. A burden shared is a burden halved. As is the case in such stories, the donkey rider thanked Javed profusely.

Looking back, Javed sometimes wondered if the poor, single donkey ever got relief. He liked to hope so. In that case, something good came out of this spontaneous street encounter. The thought of the possibility that the donkey rider went back to the market and sold the donkey haunted him at times. But he grew up believing in the goodness in people. He believed in the moment of giving, which was the moment of truth and when giving made sense. "I hope my effort counted," he thought when he remembered the encounter.

Number of Ways to Love You

"How do I love thee? Let me count the ways."
Browning left the numbers out of those lines.
The counting never began.
I wandered through her rhymes
How do I love thee? Let me number the ways.

I will hold your hands when you are frail,
I'll speak to you while you fail, to comprehend.
My care will be genuine, I will not pretend
I'll love you thus, to the core of your being

Beyond words, beyond the vision of any dream.
I'll answer your question for the fiftieth time,
I'll bathe you, change you, and clip your nails.
I'll keep your spirits high, when all else fails.

To the doctors I'll drive your wheelchair.
For my love for you, let no one else compare.
I'll cook for you and keep our kitchen clean
I'll do the dishes, check the mail, make the beds,

I'll wash, dry, and fold the clothes, sweep the floors.
To your rants or shouts, I will not be mad or be mean,
For it is you that I adore not the thought of you.
I will read the books to you, if I have a voice.

In rehab or in the ER, I'll remain by your side
I will feed you and wipe your mouth, my love.
I will defend and protect you, I will not hide
Though you act cruel, you're still my dove.

I will love thee from here until the heavens;
I will pray with you and pray for you always.
How do I love thee, let me number the ways.
When the numbers end, I'll count them again.

Let Love Wither Not

Why stay in the never-ending grind?
When all the glory is left behind
What you seek you can no longer find.
The time for us has been unkind
It is the suffering of our design.
Love brought us close in a bond
Life tied us into a twisted curvy vine
Now let reason set us free

If guilt is all that holds you
I release you of the blame,
If wealth is what you scck
I've signed all I'm worth to you

My name, in ink, is bleeding through
The pages of your writing.
The chapters closed and unrevised
The book comes out of hiding
"If you call it destiny
That fate pulled us apart,
My life is over, though I breathe.
The death now does us part."

Search for Shelter

WHEN JENNA RECEIVED the Rhodes scholarship for a research fellowship in Pakistan, she didn't realize how her life would become intertwined with one family.

Being focused on women's studies, she interviewed several local women from different walks of life. A few months into her stay in a large cosmopolitan city, she started getting used to the daily humdrum. The issues were many, and the local women had a lot to say. But her life was still within the realm of ordinary. That changed however, when she met a lady in her early thirties, Tania, with four sons and a husband who'd disappeared seven years ago. This was the family that would burrow into her heart and move her to do things that she would not have otherwise imagined. The boys were twelve, fourteen, seventeen, and eighteen. Jenna had two daughters in college in the US. She'd always wanted a son, but had never conceived one.

Tania and the boys lived in the shabbiest rental apartment. Tania worked three jobs just to keep her head above water and was failing. She barely made enough to put food on the table, had fallen behind on rent, and faced an eviction notice. When their paths crossed, Tania had ten days to leave the apartment and face the prospect of homelessness.

Tania's eighteen-year-old had left the family to live with a friend and would show up only when he had nowhere else to crash or when his friend had kicked him out. The seventeen-year-old had developed a heroin addiction. The younger ones had nothing to look forward to and no one to look up to.

Jenna felt strongly (as well as naively) that she could mobilize resources in the city to save Tania. After three days of trying, she felt the urgency of the situation and called her husband in Hartford, Connecticut. With her money, she bought a two-bedroom apartment near their community and moved the family there. She did not ask for any rent. The understanding was that Tania would stay as a relative of Jenna's and keep the apartment clean and pay for the utilities and not worry about the rent.

Tania could not believe how her luck had changed. People understand well that when no one is forcing you out onto the street, you have a chance to focus on growing your life. Once people have shelter, they feel hope again and begin to thrive.

Two years flew by, and Jenna completed her thesis and left for Connecticut. The strong ties to this family, however, brought her back year after year to check on their progress. When she'd last visited, the kids had started to take an interest in school. Tania was happily decorating the apartment and the kids were sitting down for meals as a family. All of these apparently mundane affairs brought Jenna to tears.

Over the next five years, during which the family stayed in this apartment, several things happened. The eldest son became a bit more responsible. He got married, found his calling, and became an independent young man.

Sad to say, the seventeen-year-old son did not fare so well. After several attempts at rehab, he passed away at the young age of twenty due to a drug overdose. Jenna attended the funeral and held Tania close through the range of emotions one would expect from a parent who loses a child.

Although this was an excruciatingly sad state of affairs, Tania understood that a lifetime battling addiction was not a life worth living. What's more, losing a brother to drugs acted as a strong deterrent for the younger two boys. Jenna spent considerable time with them, and knowing how the boys could benefit from discipline and a sense of purpose, she convinced Tania to have them join the Naval Academy.

Tania hesitated because of the exorbitant fees, but by this time Jenna thought of these boys as hers and funded the three-year boarding school program for both. Jenna's husband was on the board with her and helped arrange the transfer of tuition and played the role of financial guarantor.

Three years later, they both graduated successfully and prepared for careers in the Navy.

Tania was still working hard and insisted on trying to pay back some of what she'd saved to Jenna and her husband. She had one job as a sales agent at an insurance agency and another as a phlebotomist.

With the boys settling in well, Jenna encouraged Tania to renew her passport and move to Abu Dhabi for better pay and work.

Jenna knew that she could ask Tania to move out of the apartment since she no longer planned to visit the city and wanted to liquidate the investment. However, she couldn't bring herself to speak to Tania about it. *"Wouldn't that be a sort of eviction again, even if Tania is not a truly a tenant?"* she thought. It turned out that fate came again to resolve the issue amicably.

It just so happened that while waiting in line for her passport renewal, Tania met a man who helped her through the process. He turned out to be the man she would fall for. She married him, and together they opened a home health agency and moved out of Jenna's apartment into one of their own.

The wedding was simple and joyful. Jenna attended with her husband and her girls.

It was all so smooth. Jenna sold the apartment after that. It had served its purpose well. Thus, she ended a chapter of her life and her significant role in the changing landscape of a family's destiny.

Reading Jenna's thesis, one would find no mention of this family and her intimate ties that bonded her with Tania forever.

Judge and Hardship

Dear Honorable Judge, grant me US citizenship

I am an American resident, but suffering hardship;

Must I wait four more years for an American Passport?

I travel out with only my Alien identity.

At the borders I am detained, at airports I am delayed,

Questions asked of me again, why innocence must I proclaim?

'Flying...? Report to security, take fingerprints, iris scans,

Checked against a database, to answer, wait and wait,

Flights missed, commitments broken.

Do I deserve this fate?

Lectures and conferences are missions impossible.

My prestige in my field has grown over time,

A professor, a writer, a mentor, researcher, scientist,

A scholar held in esteem in the circles of influence.

Yet at the National borders, my identity is my passport,

Tainted by it, guilty by association, I am defined by it,

It robs me of my dignity, jeopardizes my plans.

My work is vital to the United States of America.

I publish and I teach, managing millions in grants,

The sickest children are under my care every day.

Yet I am treated as a felon at the airport.

That is the story I came here to share, Judge.

Palms covering his cheeks, the judge was all ears,

Distracted for a minute, his posture now straight,

Arms now folded elbows resting on the desk,

He took a while to speak, my fate hanging in the air.

And you think that is hardship?

The query stopped me in my tracks, unexpected.

I thought him to be ruthless, heartless and deaf.

What if you were a boy of only ten and had seen

What no one should have seen? Should ever see?

Your parents' blood, your parents' screams,

They're ringing loud in your ears,

Both shot dead in front of you and you run,

Slowed by the weight of your tears,

The flipping wild heart in your chest,

The burning, bursting, guts in your belly…

Canada and the US refuse to grant you home.

What would you call that if I may ask you, son?

He raised his right hand passionately speaking.

I had no words, silence besieged me entirely.

Who could top such an ultimate tragedy?

Choking on my words I said 'I am sorry judge'

I really am; the judge mellowed considerably.

As bad are our plights may seem, we're told,

Someone else has it worse, we need to trust.

"Your guts I do admire, I'd like to see that more.

Your dogged pursuit to change your plight has hit me at my core.

Craft a letter, leave nothing out, no detail should you spare.

You'll get your US passport in two years instead of four."

Honorable judge, I believe the deal is fair, I take it.

Save American Passport

Handcuffs were painful enough.
Gagging on the rope in pure delirium,
Dragged from room to room, in my own home,
Fear with intensity, barely held my piss from oozing.
One holding a gun, the other kicking me (a kicker).
'Where's your American Passport?'
This lawless land! Why am I here again?
I forgot, of course I came to get engaged;
Oh my God, would I live long enough to marry?
Let me not die at the hands of these goons!
And what do they need my passport for?
You know, photo change? Your photo out, mine in…
Some thug's picture on my passport, yikes!!
Then I go USA… ha ha ha ha', you here stay,
They say, they say;
Another closet emptied, fabric ripped apart,
Drawers pulled out roughly; one by one,
My belongings on the floor, ready for a bonfire.
By crazy luck my eyes fell on it, the passport,
The object of their desire within their grasp,
The dark blue cover—United States of America
Visible to me, but not yet to my assaulters.
I deliberately moved away from my passport.

The alarmed kicker grabbed me and threw me
Now near the passport, where I wanted to be.
My swift leg swipe pushed it deep under the bed
'*What you do, run, you … (local curses).*
Passport out of sight, I lied to my tormentors.
My passport is in the American Consulate.
Cold metal of the nozzle on my bare chest,
Colder eyes searching my eyes for truth,
Ears strain for sense in garbled words,
Kicker yanked the gag out, sore sore mouth!
Taste of blood, always unmistakable, metallic,
Hemoglobin, full of iron, distraught, angry.
I spoke again softly and humbly to the thugs:
My passport is in the American Consulate.
Swiftly, a solid metal, the gun, hits my temple.
The thud was the last sound I heard
I came to in the bathroom, handcuffed.
My body weight crashes against the door.
A neighbor on his walk looked at me in horror
In handcuffs and in gags, I reached out for help.
My car was taken, when I checked,
Carjacked, mugged, robbed, assaulted.
Worse still, I was late to celebrate, engagement.
Traumatic as it was, no time to spare to grieve,
I am living, uninjured physically,
I can dream again, I am alive!
My engagement and my life not lost
I can return to the USA, safe again at last.

My Beautiful Raindrop

The train stops, the window wakes up
A solitary raindrop slides down,
Slow, gentle, a snail-like motion.
It's full—a round, clear bubble,
Holding a window, within a window
A microcosmic landscape within.

Bushes, green meadows sliced by unused tracks, diced by trees.
The sky's blue bonnet caps its belly. Green leaves overshadow the canopy.

The boy's eyes glued to its trail.
A theatre from his seat, magnified
Where the raindrop goes,
The world in its belly glows.
The train starts, the rain-drop shivers,
Fast now, frozen. Is this the end of me?

My proud underbelly collapses
Will I last another second?
Millions of images passed through me
Yet I was hollow.
Green a tree? Blue could be the sky,
Is white the fog or cloud?
Is brown the field of dirt or the trunk of a tree?

Wind softens my grip, oblivion in the horizon.
Was I a drunken dream of a sober heart?
Did the boy create, or discover me?
Is the reflection of his vision alive inside me?
I sigh by the force of a wind.
With faith in my destiny
My wings spread into a comet,
Freedom lies amidst the possibility of doom.
The train stops, a wet globe latches on.
The boy's eyes on the raindrop trailing again
The wealth of the world in a drop of rain.
Glory of life, of magic and motion.
The rainwater speaks to the silent boy.
I will live for as long as you look at me.

You Gamble on me

A KASH HAD LEFT INDIA for the United Kingdom as a student 25 years ago. Now, he was a businessman in Australia who had achieved some success. He was thought to be in a position to help others in a similar situation.

He had barely recovered from his jet lag from a recent trip when he was asked to see if he could help a family with an eighteen-year-old girl who had secured college admission in the United States while a student in India.

It piqued his interest. He wanted to find out more. So he paid a visit to the girl at her home.

It was a modest home in an austere neighborhood. A down-to-earth mother and a mild-mannered father were raising two daughters—eighteen-year-old Anju, who was the subject of Akash's visit, and a younger sister, who was thirteen at that time. Anju was in plain clothes but could speak clearly about business and remained very courteous throughout Akash's visit.

Akash studied Anju's college acceptance letter. The instructions said to deposit $5,000 before midnight that night. She was supposed to fly out the next morning; he reviewed the flight tickets as well.

She said that she did not need money from him because her father had arranged for a loan, and it should be there in a matter of a day or two. Once it arrived, it would be transferred to the university. Akash was a bit confused as to what was expected of him.

Anju asked Akash if he would be gracious enough to serve as the guarantor for her by signing the forms and showing his Australian bank balance to cover tuition in case the loanfalters. This would help her start classes the day after next and not miss the beginning of the semester.

With a guarantor's supporting bank statements, she could at least keep moving forward.

This family was an acquaintance of an acquaintance; Akash did not know the family—he had never seen them before that day. He had no connection to them aside from the information he'd received from his acquaintance. Still, he thought this to be a low risk proposition, so he signed the financial guarantor's statement with his bank account information and left wishing the girl good luck. He thought that was easy.

He was awakened by his buzzing phone at midnight. Anju was on the other line panicking, telling him that her father's loan was delayed for at least one week. This was bad news. The university would not allow her to begin classes unless she deposited the check for $5000 as soon as she arrived.

Despite the previous assurances, the University registrar was not accepting a mere guarantor's signature anymore. She could not convince the university otherwise. Akash was flustered, cornered, and confused. He did not like to be in this kind of situation. Nobody does.

At that point, Akash needed to trust Anju, but is there any formula out there in the world to build a trust after a few hours of knowing someone?

"Anju, can I really, really trust you that I will get my money back from your father after you leave?" He decided to take the most direct approach. "Tell me honestly what is happening here."

She explained very patiently that in the absence of this money, she would have to cancel the flight and lose the money on her tickets. She'd also have to wait a semester at home and be at the mercy of the college to honor her admission offer the following semester. To further complicate her situation, her fate would be determined by the US Visa and Immigration office to grant her visa again at that time. She would require an entirely new visa application.

If she took the flight anyway and moved to the United States, she would be a burden to some distant relatives. She'd have to wait for three months doing odd jobs to support herself in the US, which might not even be possible under newer visa rules.

Akash gave her the check for $5,000, and she departed the very next day.

Luckily, this was one of those happy-ending stories. The father personally visited Akash with the repayment check repeatedly offering his gratitude.

As far as Anju was concerned, she made the most of her studies and good fortune to be studying in the US. She achieved top grades in her school. She finished her undergrad degree from Boston University and went on to pursue graduate studies. In the process, she found the love of her life and got married.

Now, she has a beautiful baby and supports her sister, who also recently finished her undergrad studies.

The parents were able to make it to their graduations and visited several times thereafter. For years following, Anju sent email messages thanking Akash repeatedly until he asked her to stop thanking him.

Akash was happy about how everything had worked out for Anju. It was a good gamble, after all. He was so glad he had some role in her route to success.

Golden Years

Rich experiences, knowledge,
Some wealth perhaps as well.
A lifetime of wisdom, advantage,
A presence of value, why farewell?

So much to give and so little time.
Why sit on the laurels and hide?
The youth is always in its prime
Yet wisdom will not hurt their pride.

There are hearts to free of fear
There are other buckets to be filled
There are hands to held so tight
There are lands to be tilled.

Golden, yes, but years there are more
While the urge to live still exists.
Let's bring other souls to shore
Embrace all life and do not desist.

Accepting Death Before Sixty

Fifty years of life is all you need,
My grandpa would often whisper,
Half to study, half to work and play.
Your landmark research is complete,
Your marriage and honeymoon too.
Your children grown up now,
Lads and ladies in your life,
Your career moved as far as it could,
Your finances are in order,
The mortgage less than half
You can die in peace, over fifty.
Not convinced? Here is more.
You've helped the youth along
You've mentored your students well
Altruistically, charitably, selflessly
You advocated your truth,
While voting, petitioning,
In some instances, protesting.
Dined in the best of restaurants,
You've travelled the world all over
You've read the best-selling books,
Watched the greatest plays on earth.
Seems your work in the world is done
The life insurance will feed your folks.

A terminal disease, or an incurable illness,

A fatal crash, or a cardiac shock

Can save you from future years of hell.

The D of death is sanctity from the terrible Ds

That longevity brings upon us:

Debility, Deafness, Depression

Dementia, Dependence, Desolation

Distanced children and Diseases

That linger on and on for years.

Don't pity the young who die;

Let people envy the ones who got away,

Escaped what most of us are destined for:

Retirement plan, Estate plan, Assisted living,

Lose one faculty after another, wait for unknown,

Driver's license? Gone; spouse? Gone,

Money? Not sure; Mobility? Gone.

New best friends? Doctors and therapists.

What you've done by fifty matters.

The rest is fluff at best, meaningless at worst.

Curbside Manners

She waved at me but I,

For my distracted senses,

Couldn't lift a finger in response;

I stopped for people to cross.

Inside my car, the rhythm was fast,

Left hand on the steering wheel

Right foot on the brake

Right hand checks the email.

Phone with its ever-urgent needs…

I barely lift my eyes,

Bowed head in allegiance,

Cursory glances with squinted eyes,

Red light and school children, many.

Click, swap, enter, swap, mail check…

The entourage passes, slowly.

Side glances, low battery, hook again,

Green, go go go, someone waves;

I drive my car away

To somewhere more important than

Waving back to crossing kids

Learning to navigate their world.

One with a sweet smile thanks me;

I realize a second too late, her wave,

Her earnest wave, I've foolishly missed.

Red light should mean look up and wave.

Trading Pants

In a matter of minutes, the doors will shut.

My dream of meeting my celebrity will die.

So close, but the entrance is denied.

The dress code bars me from the meeting I desire.

I am frantic, desperate, as I ask the folks around me,

Sir, I will stand in the back, no one would mind me.

You need long pants man; your shorts won't do

Cameras and crowds gather, anticipating the limo.

I ran into a man my size out on the street

'Could you please exchange your pants with mine?'

He was taken aback, aghast, speechless in anger,

Ten dollars I offered, to entice him for his pants.

He was now beyond anger, hurt in fact.

Do you think of me a fool sir? His face flushed,

My explanation was Greek to him, it seemed in vain.

My deed was beyond foolish, I checked myself in pain,

Composed later in reflection, dreadfully stupid,

Cannot buy a man's dignity, intent notwithstanding.

I felt sorrow, the memory is still vivid, lucid,

Hilarious it sounds years later, yet it still stings

A tale of insanity in pursuit of celebrity spins.

Notes from the Author

Thank you for your interest in this book. I hope you enjoyed it. Please leave a review on Amazon.com or goodreads.com.

Your reviews keep the book alive and in circulation. If you don't have an Amazon.com account, then kindly leave the review on goodreads.com. It would be deeply appreciated.

Please visit *authorsaal.com*

Thank you and warm regards,

Saal Baraan

Biography

Saal Baraan is the pen name of published writer, author, poet, professor, and physician, Dr. Sulaiman Bharwani. His book, *Of Myriad Paths,* garnered numerous positive reviews and several awards. It was the recipient of an "Editor's Pick" award badge by Huge Orange (hugeorange.com) and received 4 out of 4 stars on onlinebookclub.org. It was a Number 1 Amazon Best Seller in the free books' category on poetry about death in October 2019.

Wind in the Flute is a collection of tales of giving and the lessons learned, expressed in prose and prose poetry. It is enriched by beautiful sketch illustrations. Dr. Bharwani speaks of opportunities of being generous with ourselves and with people who come into our lives. Their presence is often for a reason or for a lesson.

Dr. Bharwani lives in Michigan with his wife and two daughters. He enjoys taking long walks and reading when he is not busy seeing patients, teaching medical students and residents, or reviewing cases requiring an expert witness. Dr. Bharwani is a strong proponent of blending the medium of writing and illustrations. You can get his books here:

https://www.amazon.com/Myriad-Paths-resilience-tenacity-hope-ebook/dp/B07V4N54XR

or at

www.authorsaal.com

www.ingramcontent.com/pod-product-compliance
Lightning Source LLC
Chambersburg PA
CBHW031341060726

47590CB00007B/2582